FLYING FERGUS

The
Photo Finish

First published in Great Britain in 2019 by
Piccadilly Press
80-81 Wimpole Street, London, W1G 9RE
www.piccadillypress.co.uk

A CIP catalogue record for this book is available from the British Library.

ISBN: 978-1-848-12642-8
also available as an ebook

1 3 5 7 9 10 8 6 4 2

Typeset in OpenDyslexic-Alta
bound by Clays Ltd, Elcograf S.p.A.

FLYING FERGUS

The
Photo Finish

CHRIS HOY
with Joanna Nadin

Illustrations by Clare Elsom

Piccadilly
PRESS

CONTENTS

Chapter 1
The Biscuit Baron is Back   1

Chapter 2
The Bonkers Banana Ban   17

Chapter 3
Butts Are for Sitting On   33

Chapter 4
Silent Bicycles and Sit-Ins   47

Chapter 5
The Manchester Grand   63

Chapter 6
Place Your Bets   79

Chapter 7
Ruler for a Day   93

Chapter 8
The International Finish Line   115

Chapter 9
Two of a Kind   137

Meet Fergus
and his friends...

Chimp

Fergus

Grandpa Herc

Daisy

Jambo Patterson

Mum

Mikey McLeod

Minnie McLeod

Wesley Wallace

Calamity Coogan

Dermot Eggs

Sorcha

Charlie Campbell

Choppy Wallace

Belinda Bruce

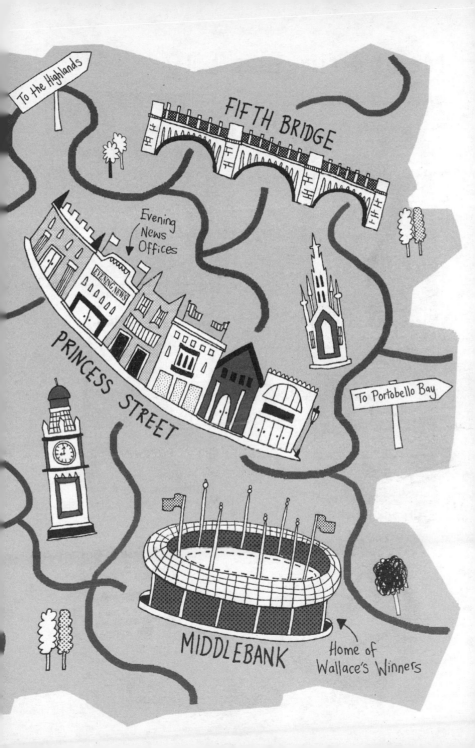

Meet Princess Lily

and her friends...

Hector Hamilton

Princess Lily

Unlucky Luke

Percy the Pretty Useless

Demelza

Douglas

Dimmock

King Woebegot

Prince Waldorf

Queen Woebegot

Duke Dastardly

Prince Derek

Knights of No Nonsense

Scary Mary

Chapter 1

The Biscuit Baron is Back

Fergus Hamilton was an ordinary nine-year-old boy. He liked monkeys (especially when they sat on Jambo's van and stole sandwiches In the safari park), bumble bees (except when they got inside Jambo's van and buzzed too close to him), and woolly mammoths (although they were extinct, which was a relief for Jambo's van, at least).

He didn't like big dogs (because they scared his own mongrel, Chimp), or wasps (because they were useless), and he definitely didn't like dinosaurs (because they scared him, even if they were extinct).

Yes, he was ordinary in almost every way, except one. Because, for a small boy, Fergus Hamilton had an extraordinarily big imagination.

Some days he imagined he lived next door to Captain Gadget, his favourite comic book character, who would spot Fergus's potential and train him up as a superhero sidekick to share in his adventures.

Some days he imagined he lived round the corner from Steve "Spokes" Sullivan, his favourite sporting hero, who would take him under his wing and coach him to become a cycling world champion one day, just like Spokes had been.

And some days he imagined he lived down the road from his dad, his real hero, so they could spend more time discussing tactics for the Palace Pedallers, the team they both looked after in the parallel universe of Nevermore.

But this morning Fergus was imagining he lived in the same city as his best friend Daisy. He couldn't believe she'd had to move all the way to Inverness for her dad's job. And just before the International Championships as well. Sorcha, his second-best friend, was great, and his team-mates cheered him up no end, but Fergus missed Daisy every minute of every day.

And he missed her most right
now, what with all the hoo-hah at
Hopefuls' HQ.

"What do you mean, you're stepping
up?" Grandpa asked Mr Bruce.
Belinda's dad, the biggest biscuit
baron in five counties, was the
official sponsor of the Hercules'
Hopefuls cycle team. "No one asked
anyone to step anywhere. Did we,
Choppy?"

Choppy shook his head. "I'm as
baffled as you are, Herc."

"Not the point," boomed Mr Bruce.
"It's my name on the team jerseys
and I want in."

"But you've already got in," said Grandpa. "You said it yourself. Your name is on the jerseys."

"And the water bottles," added Fergus, checking out the slogan in bright red on the side of his own: *Bruce's Biscuits, bringing home winners.*

"And the helmets," added Calamity.

"And the minibus," said Minnie with a sigh. "Which is a worry. What if we don't win? Then you'll be bringing home losers."

"Not if I get my way," barked Mr Bruce.

"And what *is* your way exactly?" asked Grandpa.

"Yes, do tell us," said Choppy. "We're all ears."

Fergus and the gang fell silent as they waited. Belinda seemed extremely nervous about what might come out of her dad's mouth. And when he spoke, it was obvious why.

"I want to be coach," said Mr Bruce.

Fergus's jaw dropped open. "You've got to be joking!" he said.

"Aye, we've two coaches already," said Grandpa. "And neither of us is going anywhere, are we, Choppy?"

Choppy shook his head. "Not on your Nellie," he agreed.

"I don't mean head coach," Mr Bruce said. "Or even second head," he added, looking at Grandpa.

Fergus felt himself bristle at the suggestion Grandpa was second-best. Grandpa and Choppy were equal on the team – they all were.

But some, it seemed, were more equal than others.

"I'll be Executive Coach," said Mr Bruce.

"Executive Coach?" asked Wesley. "What's one of those when it's at home?"

Mr Bruce smiled – a sort of super-villain smile, Fergus thought to himself, wishing again that Captain Gadget lived next door.

"It means," said Mr Bruce. "That I am top dog."

Chimp whimpered.

"Of course it does," muttered Choppy, as he and Grandpa raised their eyebrows at each other.

"I won't be actually on the track," continued Mr Bruce, "more in the boardroom. But I'll be in charge

of tactics for these last few days
before the Internationals. We need
to get ahead of the game, after all."

"It's not a game," Fergus found
himself blurting out loud. "It's a
sport."

"Sport, game, whatever," said Mr
Bruce. "But that's the deal. Take it
or leave it. If you leave it, though,
I'll be having my minibus back. And
the car stickers. And the novelty
pen toppers."

Then Mr Bruce crossed his arms,
waiting, Fergus assumed, for the
answer "yes". How could Grandpa
and Choppy refuse, if it meant
they'd lose the sponsorship money?

Instead of saying "yes", though, Grandpa said, "Give us a minute," sending Fergus's hopes soaring. "We need a team talk. I'm sure given your . . . devotion to the Hopefuls, you understand how important that is."

"I don't –" blustered Mr Bruce.

But Belinda interrupted. "Please, Daddy. We'll only be a moment." She smiled sweetly – a smile that Fergus just knew was all ploy.

It worked.

"Fine," said Mr Bruce, clearly
unable to refuse his darling daughter
anything. "You can have one minute.
But one minute only, understand?
And I'll be right outside."

"You've got it, Daddy," said
Belinda, a little too quickly for
Fergus's liking. But maybe she had
another trick up her sleeve. Or two?

But as soon as the door was shut,
it was clear that no one had any
tricks, or even ideas.

"Do we really need novelty pen-
toppers?" asked Mikey. "Or even
helmets? Well, obviously we need
helmets."

"Especially in my case," said Calamity.

Mikey nodded with a half-smile. "What I meant was, do we need slogans on them? We've managed without that so far."

"It's more the minibus I'm worried about," admitted Grandpa. "How do we get to the Internationals without it? It's a long way to Manchester, and we need to take all our bikes and kit."

"And what about when we get there?" said Choppy. "Mr Bruce is stumping up the cash for the hotel and without that, where are we going to kip?"

"Tents?" suggested Fergus.

"Are you mad?" asked Wesley.
"I'm not sleeping in a tent. We can
sleep in the minibus."

"Yeah, minibus," said Dermot.

"But we won't *have* the minibus,"
Grandpa reminded them.

"Oh, yeah," said Wesley, gloomy again.

Fergus had an idea. "Can't you talk to him?" he asked Belinda. "He's your dad, he'll listen to you."

But Belinda shook her head. "I don't think he will. I told him I didn't want a pony for my birthday, or a parakeet. I'd have been happy with a hamster. But now I have Tallulah and Tarquin, and I'm allergic to both of them!"

Grandpa sighed. "There's nothing for it," he said. "Choppy?"

Choppy nodded reluctantly. "Fine. Mr Bruce as Executive Coach it is. We'll just have to cross our fingers and hope he doesn't actually *have* any bright ideas."

Fergus crossed his fingers and his toes, too. But as Grandpa went out to give Mr Bruce the good (or bad) news, Fergus had a funny feeling that this wasn't going to end well.

No, not well at all.

Chapter 2

The Bonkers Banana Ban

Not for the first time that morning,
Fergus wished Daisy was by his side.

It was bad enough that Mr Bruce
had been named Executive Coach,
but apparently he actually *did*
have some bright ideas – although
"bright" was not the word Fergus
would use to describe them.

"A banana ban?" Fergus asked

incredulously. "But why?"

Mr Bruce puffed out his chest.
"Well, I knew you'd ask that, so I've
made a little presentation for you."

Fergus glanced at Belinda, who
rolled her eyes.

"Lights off," demanded Mr Bruce,
as he unfurled a screen and flicked
on a projector. "This is how we do
things in big business," he boomed.

"Aye, all flash and no substance,"
muttered Grandpa.

Fergus and Belinda smiled. But
only for a second, because as soon
as the film started rolling, the
whole team had their mouths agape.

"So you see," said Mr Bruce when it had ended. "Bananas are too simple. They're perfectly fine for monkeys in the wild, but not for men in the twenty-first century."

"What about women?" Belinda asked indignantly.

"Of course, my precious little princess." Mr Bruce smiled. "No bananas for you either."

"That's not what I –" Belinda began.

But Mr Bruce shut her up quick. "So, 'What's the alternative?' I hear you asking."

"I wasn't asking," whispered Wesley.

"Nor me," said Fergus.

But they were going to be told anyway.

"Biscuits!" proclaimed Mr Bruce, producing a packet from his jacket pocket with a flourish.

"Mmm, biscuits," repeated Dermot.

"Exactly," said Mr Bruce. "And the thing about these beauties is that they're packed with special man-made ingredients that are designed to give you energy fast, which, let's face it, you need at speed."

"Packed with lots of sugar, you mean," said Grandpa.

"Mmm, sugar," repeated Dermot.

"Bananas have sugar but they release their energy slowly, that's the whole point," said Fergus, remembering one of Daisy's top facts. "So we don't get a dip."

"Eat enough of *these* biscuits and you'll not sleep in weeks," said Mr Bruce, handing out packets to everyone from a gigantic box. "Bouncing off the walls, you'll be."

Fergus looked at Grandpa in disbelief. Mr Bruce surely couldn't be suggesting that the best diet for the International Cycle Championships was – Fergus squinted at the packet – Bruce's Butterscotch Bonanzas. Could he?

"That's right, munch up," said Mr Bruce as Dermot tore into the packet and stuffed several in his mouth at once.

Grandpa shrugged. It seemed that as Executive Coach and sponsor of the team, Mr Bruce could. And that wasn't all.

"I've another change to announce," said Mr Bruce, brushing crumbs off his own pin-striped suit.

"There's going to be a switch in who wears the Number One jersey."

Fergus, who was already feeling queasy from the smell of so many butterscotch biscuits, felt his stomach slide like he was about to be sick. Mr Bruce couldn't mess with placings, surely? Number One jersey was always him or Wesley, and the final choice should be down to Grandpa and Choppy, not this newcomer who knew nothing about their track record.

But again, Fergus was about to find out just how wrong he was.

"From now on," continued Mr Bruce, "my baby Belinda will be riding out front. She's my champion and she should be yours as well."

Belinda shook her head. "But, Daddy!" she protested. "I don't –"

"Nonsense," her father interrupted. "You deserve it, sweetheart."

"For what?" asked Belinda, baffled.

"For being my beautiful Belinda, of course." Mr Bruce smiled widely and indulgently.

"Now hang on . . . " began Fergus.

"But that's so . . . " said Wesley at the same time.

But Mr Bruce silenced them both.
"I'll not hear another word on the
subject."

Or rather, he tried to silence
them. Because Fergus found his
anger had quelled his funny tummy
and was bubbling up inside like hot
lava instead. Yes, he was a one-boy
volcano and he was about to erupt.

"How dare you?" Fergus
demanded. "No offence to Belinda,
who's brilliant by the way, but
Wesley's better, and he deserves
that place."

"No, Fergus does," argued Wesley
quickly, quite to Fergus's (and
everyone else's) surprise.

But Fergus didn't stop. "You can feed us all the biscuits you want, Mr Bruce, but Wesley's times are up on mine so he's our number one. Not Belinda, and not me. And that's final." He crossed his arms and stared at Mr Bruce.

Mr Bruce stared hard back at Fergus, his face reddening by the second.

"Are you *arguing* with me, boy?"

Fergus glanced at Grandpa, hoping
for back-up. Grandpa nodded.

Fergus found his voice again. "Well
. . . yes, I suppose I am."

Mr Bruce paused for a moment,
looking so disgusted it was almost
as if he thought that Fergus was dog
poo on the bottom of his shoe. Then
he spoke, slowly and deliberately
and damningly.

"In that case, boy, you are off the
team entirely."

Fergus gasped.

Everyone else gulped.

"This boy – what's his name?" Mr Bruce pointed at Dermot, still stuffing his face with Butterscotch Bonanzas.

"Dermot?" said Wesley, horrified.

"Me?" Dermot spluttered crumbs everywhere.

"Yes, Dermot," said Mr Bruce, pleased. "He seems to agree with my policies. He can take your place. And if anyone else so much as murmurs, they'll be replaced as well."

With that as his final word, Mr Bruce stalked from the room.

Wesley snapped his mouth shut, as did everyone else. Even Chimp.

Fergus felt his legs turn to wet, wobbly jelly. So much for being a fiery boy volcano. It couldn't be true, could it? Off the team for the Internationals – the most important cycling championships they'd ever qualified for?

But it seemed he really was.

"I'm sorry, sonny," said Grandpa,
placing a hand on his shoulder.

"What can I do?" whispered
Fergus, his voice fading as fast as
his hopes.

Grandpa shook his head.
"I honestly don't know. We'll
fix it somehow, you can be sure
of that. But for now, you're going
to have to play along."

"Play along?"

"Aye," said Grandpa. "For now, at least. Like a big game of 'Let's Pretend'. You can manage that, can't you?"

Fergus nodded. Imagination was his strong point, he knew that.

But this wasn't just make-believe. This was the future of Hercules' Hopefuls.

And Fergus wasn't even in it.

Chapter 3

Butts Are for Sitting On

"Och, Fergie, I cannae believe it,"
said Mum, when he trudged in and
slumped on the sofa, Chimp at his
feet. "Herc told us what happened
with Mr Bruce."

"He's got no right," added Jambo.
"No right at all. Herc, surely you can
sort it?"

Fergus turned to Grandpa again,

but he just held up his hands.

"Unless we can come up with another source of sponsorship, there's nothing any of us can do," Grandpa said. "We need money to pay for the minibus and the hotel in Manchester. So for now we just have to sit it out and wait for Mr Bruce to come to his senses."

"It won't take long if everyone's burning through biscuits and running out of juice," said Jambo. "They'll fall off before they hit the finish line."

"Don't you believe it," said Fergus. "Dermot can eat a whole packet of Bruce's Juicy Lucys on the move."

"That's not even legal," said Jambo. "Hang on. I should run this as a story, Herc! *Boy Champion Deposed Over Butterscotch Biscuit Row.* What do you say? People power will push Mr Bruce to do the right thing, surely?"

But Grandpa shook his head. "And have us show up at Internationals a laughing stock?"

"We'll be a laughing stock anyway if we carry on like this," said Fergus grimly.

But Grandpa was insistent. "We'll sort it out from inside the team," he said. "You focus on the wedding, Jambo. It's only a few days after Manchester, after all."

"Och, okay," said Jambo. "I'm certainly busy enough at the Evening News and writing articles for the Herald too."

"Aye," said Mum. "I'm working all hours at the moment to save up a bit extra and what with . . ." She stopped.

"What?" asked Fergus.

Mum and Jambo exchanged a
glance. "Nothing," they said.

Fergus felt his insides slop and
slide for the second time that day.
"Is something wrong?" he asked.

Mum shook her head. "Definitely
not," she said, then changed the
subject sharpish. "Now, why don't
you go and have a bath and then
give Daisy a quick ring? She left
a message earlier."

Fergus's found himself managing to smile at this news – he'd been dying to speak to Daisy, and now more than ever. So without even trying to argue, he clattered along the hallway and into the bathroom, where he washed, spruced and pulled on clean togs, before settling down in the hallway holding the telephone in one hand and stroking Chimp with the other.

"Mr Bruce did what?" demanded Daisy after Fergus had filled her in.

"I've told you twice now," Fergus said. "And it's still the same. He sacked me!"

"But he can't," came the outraged reply.

"But he did," Fergus batted back. "And that's not all. Something's going on with Mum and Jambo."

"The wedding, that's what," said Daisy. "Weddings turn everyone doolally. Unless . . . "

"Unless what?" Fergus asked.

"Well, you don't suppose they're thinking of moving, are they?"

"What do you mean? Who's moving?"

"Your mum and Jambo, of course!" said Daisy. "I mean, you can't all stay in that flat."

"Why can't we?" said Fergus.

But Daisy was too busy thinking
to listen. "Maybe Jambo's got a
new job," she said. "Maybe it's in
Inverness!"

For a moment Fergus let himself
imagine living near Daisy again. They
could set up a new team together.
But then, he'd miss this place too
much. And he'd miss the Hopefuls.
Even though they weren't really his
team right now.

"I don't think so," Fergus said.
"They'd tell me if we were moving."

But even as he said it, he wasn't
so sure. Anything could happen to
the Hamiltons, it seemed, so moving
miles away wasn't completely out
of the question. If Daisy's mum
and dad had moved, then it wasn't
impossible, was it?

"I wish you were here," he said to
Daisy then.

"I wish you were here, Fergie!"
Daisy said immediately. "I really
miss you and all the team. But I
have had a bit of luck – I met some

kids at the park, Jack and Ryan, who are into cycling too, and they invited me to try out for their team, the Inverness Arrows. They're identical twins so I need a bit of help telling them apart but luckily their bikes are different colours." Daisy paused. "What about Sorcha – isn't she around?"

"She's in the Hebrides on holiday," said Fergus with a sigh. "Back the day before the last race in Manchester. Not that I'll be racing," he added.

"Listen," Daisy said. "Moping around's not going to do you any good."

"So what *do* I do?" asked Fergus.

"You do what you always do when you fall off. You get back in the saddle. And you get cycling."

"What for?" asked Fergus.

"What for?" repeated Daisy. "Are you serious? Because otherwise you're just letting Mr Bruce and his stupid butterscotch biscuits win."

"Maybe," said Fergus.

"Not maybe," said Daisy. "Definitely. And no biscuits. Get back on the bananas so you're fighting fit when he realises his mistake."

"Okay," said Fergus, brightening slightly.

"And no buts either," added Daisy. "Because . . . "

"Butts are for sitting on," said Fergus, finally finding a smile.

"You bet they are!" said Daisy. "I'm going to train with the twins for the Arrows tryouts, and I want a full report from you on the Hopefuls."

"You'll get one," Fergus promised.

And so excited was he by Daisy's pep talk that he almost forgot to say goodbye to her before he put down the phone and fled through the kitchen in the direction of the front door.

"Hey, what's the hurry?" asked

Jambo. "I thought you were going to help with last-minute wedding prep. You need to make sure that mutt fits his bow-tie for a start!"

Chimp yelped.

Fergus's face fell. "But Internationals start in three days," he pointed out. "I need to practice."

"Good work, sonny," said Grandpa, nodding in approval.

"Aye, go on, scram," said Mum, smiling. "I'm glad your chat with Daisy helped and you're seeing the sunny side again."

"But what about tea?" asked Jambo. "I've done spaghetti."

"Can I have it cold later?" Fergus asked.

"Och, have something now," said Mum. "You need the energy. Just a little biscuit?"

Fergus grinned. "Better than that," he said, grabbing a piece of fruit from the bowl. "I'll have a banana."

And peeling it as he went, Fergus set off in high spirits and with high hopes. He couldn't change the Biscuit Baron's mind. Not yet, anyway. But he *could* look after himself. And that was exactly what he was going to do.

Chapter 4

Silent Bicycles and Sit-Ins

Boosted by his brilliant training spin the night before, Fergus kept his promise to Daisy and turned up to practice promptly in the morning.

But within minutes he felt his winning attitude waning and his resolve dissolving like the sugar on top of a Bruce's Bubblegum Bake.

Fergus nudged Belinda. "Who's

that?" he asked, nodding at the short, stubby man standing next to her dad.

"No idea," she replied. "Dad doesn't tell me anything."

"I know," said Calamity, frowning. "It's Pete Prowse."

"What? Pete 'Pedals' Prowse?" asked Wesley, aghast. "But, isn't he . . . "

Calamity nodded.

"Inventor of the Silent Bicycle?" said Mr Bruce. "Yes, he is. And he's invented a model just for us."

"Hang on," said Choppy. "Aren't Silent Bicycles —"

"Motor-powered?" interrupted Mr Bruce. "Yes, they are."

"Wait," said Grandpa. "Motors? So you don't actually have to use any effort at all?"

"Bingo!" said Mr Bruce. "The motors Pedals Prowse has fixed up for us will slip inside the spokes and the . . . the . . . whatever those twirly things are, and because they're silent and now invisible, no one will be any the wiser."

"Let me get this straight," said Grandpa slowly. "You're saying you want us to use motorized bicycles?

At the International Championships?
In front of a crowd of thousands?"

"Again, bingo!" said Mr Bruce.
"You're quite the brainbox, after
all."

"Steady on," said Grandpa.

But Mr Bruce wasn't going to go
steady or slow down either. "It's
guaranteed success!" he declared.
"No one will beat us with our secret
engines on board. Not the Brisbane
Blethers. Not even the Shanghai
Shenaniflops."

"The Brisbane Belters," corrected
Grandpa. "And the Shanghai
Shooting Stars. But that's not the
point. The point is, that's *cheating!*"

"I know!" agreed Mr Bruce happily. "Genius, isn't it?"

"Choppy?" Grandpa turned to him. "Back me up here. Remember what happened when you fiddled with our bikes before a big race?"

Choppy nodded. "Aye," he said. "But with these secret engines we're not sabotaging any one else's equipment, or chances?"

"It would give us the edge," Wesley said, and Mikey nodded in agreement.

Fergus couldn't believe what he was hearing. "No!" he snapped. "We . . . we just can't. Because even if it did work and we did win, it wouldn't be a real victory." He turned to Wesley and Mikey. "Don't you want to feel what it's like to cross the finishing line at the Internationals under your own steam?"

Wesley hesitated. "Yes, but –"

"No buts, Wesley," continued Fergus, fired up again. "Butts are for sitting on! We just won't do it, Mr Bruce."

"Oh, really?" Mr Bruce replied. "And how do you plan to stop it, exactly?"

Fergus smiled: the famous Sorcha Henderson Sit-In! It had worked on Daisy when she had refused to talk to him, so it would work on Mr Bruce too.

"We'll refuse to race until you take back the secret engines and end the banana ban," Fergus announced triumphantly, sitting down and crossing his arms and legs in defiance.

"But you're not even on the team," scoffed Mr Bruce. "Get up and stop being silly, little boy."

Fergus looked at his team-mates. Come on, he willed them silently. But Mikey was avoiding his eye, and Wesley was examining the spokes on his bike wheel. He glanced at Grandpa in despair.

And that's when it happened.

"But I'm on the team," said Belinda, sitting down next to Fergus and crossing her arms and legs too. "I'm on the team, and I refuse to race."

Calamity sat swiftly, if unsteadily, next. "I'm on the team," he repeated. "And I refuse to race!"

Minnie was next, and then Mikey, followed by Wesley and, finally, Dermot, who would have been quicker but was looking for a lost biscuit in his kit bag.

Then, to Fergus's delight, Grandpa sat down too. And so did Choppy.

"I think that's unanimous, Mr Bruce," Choppy said. "It's normal bicycles. And Fergus is right, you can drop the banana ban and take back the biscuits too. If I see another Bruce's Butterscotch Bonanza you'll be seeing my breakfast."

"But . . . but . . ." blustered Mr Bruce. "What about the minibus? And the hotel in Manchester? It'll be tents in the Arndale Shopping Centre for you without my sponsorship money!"

"No, it won't," came a voice.

Fergus swivelled on his bottom to see Jambo walk in.

"Patterson," snorted Mr Bruce. "And what's your plan? Are you going to tell the truth in your terrible newspaper? Ooh, I'm quaking in my shoes."

Jambo rolled his eyes. "No," he said. "Like Herc has already pointed out to me, the team would be a laughing stock if we made all this biscuit bother public. But the paper does come into it."

"How?" asked Fergus.

"Meet your new sponsor!" announced Jambo, unrolling a new Number One jersey and handing it to Belinda. But this time, instead of BRUCE'S BISCUITS emblazoned on the back, it read:

"Well, a jersey's one thing," sneered Mr Bruce. "But don't tell me they've stumped up for a minibus as well."

"Oh, aye," Jambo confirmed. "And helmets, and water bottles, and novelty pen-toppers, and the hotel bill in Manchester, so there'll be no tents. Not unless you're planning on joining us, that is. I think everywhere else is booked up."

"Belinda?" blurted Mr Bruce. "Do something!"

But Belinda shook her head. "I'm with Fergus," she said.

"But I was going to rename the team in your honour," her dad insisted. "The Brilliant Belindas."

To Fergus's relief and delight, Belinda didn't care. "I'm a Hercules' Hopeful," she said. "And this can go back to its rightful owner as well."

Belinda held the Number One jersey out to Fergus.

"Really?" he asked.

"Really," she answered. "You're the best leader this team has."

Fergus looked around to see Grandpa and Choppy nodding, and the rest of the Hopefuls smiling too. Their smiles were so wide, he could ignore Mr Bruce's blistering glare.

"Take it," urged Wesley. "You deserve it."

Fergus took a deep breath, then took the jersey. "I'll do everything I can," he said seriously. Then, jumping to his feet, a grin breaking over his face, he yelled the words he'd been holding in for months now:

"Manchester, here we come!"

Chapter 5

The Manchester Grand

"Are you sure you've got everything?"
Mum asked, for what seemed to
Fergus like the eleventy-billionth time.

"I'm sure," he replied.

"Are you sure you're sure?" she
said.

Fergus rolled his eyes. "Muuuu-
uuuum!"

"Och, okay, okay. But it's my job to worry."

"You wouldn't need to worry if you were coming with us," said Fergus, failing to hide his disappointment.

"Fergie, we've been through this," said Mum. "There's work tonight, then there's everything left to do before the wedding and I . . . well, you'll understand soon enough."

"Understand what?" Fergus asked suspiciously.

"Soon," repeated Mum.

Fergus couldn't believe this. The biggest event of his life and no one was coming to watch him race. Daisy lived too far away now. Sorcha wasn't back from holiday yet. But Mum not coming was the worst. He turned to Jambo, desperate. "Can't you drive back and fetch Mum, just so she can see me race?"

Jambo shook his head. "Och, there won't be time, Fergie. But you'll have Grandpa and Chimp. And . . . well, I know it's not the same but you'll have me too." He put a hand on Fergus's shoulder.

The weight of it felt good, and
Fergus nodded, finding a smile.
Jambo was right, it wasn't the same,
but he'd have his support, and
Chimp and Grandpa too.

And all his team-mates, of course.
They were all sharing rooms at
the Manchester Grand. At that
thought, Fergus began to brim with
excitement. He was still sad about
Mum not making it, but . . . a hotel?
In a different city? And then there
was the championship itself . . .

Fergus decided that it was time
to buck up. These were going to be
the biggest races of his life, and
he was jolly well going to have the
time of his life.

"Ready?" asked Jambo. "Your grandpa's just loading the minibus, then we'll fetch the others."

Fergus nodded. "I'm ready," he replied, his smile widening into a grin. "Ready for anything."

And he'd never meant it more.

If the drive to Manchester in the
new minibus was a blast, the hotel
itself was out of this world. On
the ground floor of the Manchester
Grand there was a super-smart
restaurant with white tablecloths
and silver cutlery, where the team
would eat their specially prepared
breakfasts. In the basement was a
swimming pool – although that was
strictly out of bounds until after
the races, Choppy said. But it was
upstairs in their shared bedrooms
that Fergus and his friends were
really blown away.

In every room was a stack of the
latest cycling magazines, goodie

bags packed with "Manchester Internationals" baseball caps, jerseys and even socks, a TV tuned to fourteen different sports channels and, best of all, a special bed just for Chimp in Fergus's room. Not that Chimp wanted to sleep in it with so many other beds to choose from.

"You can bunk up with me, Chimp," Wesley encouraged the dog, clicking his fingers.

"No, me!" demanded Dermot,
wiggling a biscuit.

"What about me?" called Mikey
from the adjoining room on the right,
where he was sharing with Calamity.

"I don't think so." Minnie looked
out from behind the left-hand door.
"Chimp wants to sleep with us.

Our room is far nicer, isn't it, B?"

"Well, obviously." Belinda
appeared next to her. "Because we
have a foot spa, a fancy hairdryer
and a mini-fridge with fruit in it."

"And we don't?" asked Wesley,
pointing to his feet, which were
already soaking in scented bubbles.

"Lovely," said a voice from the doorway.

Fergus turned to see Choppy standing with his hands on his hips and Grandpa and Jambo behind him with frowns on their faces.

"It's all very well having feet that smell like a flowerbed," began Choppy, "but sleep's what you need, and a good eight hours of it at least."

"Aye," agreed Grandpa. "So everyone back to their own beds – that includes you, Chimp."

Reluctantly, Chimp hopped off Fergus's bunk.

"And lights out in ten minutes," added Jambo. "Tomorrow's a big day, so let's make sure we rise to the occasion."

"But we need to talk tactics," insisted Wesley. "And . . ." he picked up a packet from the dressing table "'rejuvenate our skin with a mixture of avocado oil and lemon peel.'"

Grandpa shook his head. "Save the team talk for the breakfast table," he said. "And save the face cream for Fergie's mum. Jeanie could use a bit of pampering."

Fergus felt a bit funny hearing that. What did he mean? Was something up with Mum? Or did Grandpa just mean pampering for the wedding?

"Come on now," said Choppy, shaking the thoughts from Fergus's head. "Bed."

"Aye, empty your minds and try to dream sweet," said Grandpa.

Reluctantly the gang slipped back to their own rooms and under their own duvets. And, after only another hour of whispering about their Shanghai rivals, who were favourites to take the title, one by one the Hercules' Hopefuls emptied their heads and drifted off to sleep.

Well, all except Fergus.

Because something was bothering him, a thought – or thoughts, really – buzzing around like persistent bees. He'd tried to push them away but they just kept zooming back. There was Mum, for a start, and the mystery of what was up with her. Then there was the fact that neither Mum nor Daisy or even Sorcha could come to cheer him on when the others all had someone coming specially to support them. Minnie and Mikey had their mum and dad. Calamity had his gran. Dermot had his Uncle Eggs. Wesley had his Aunt Wallace. Even Mr Bruce was coming to see Belinda, though Fergus was pretty sure he'd bring biscuits and the parakeet, just to annoy her.

No, Fergus was the only one on his own out there. Jambo and Grandpa and Chimp weren't the same – they *had* to be there. No matter how hard he tried to tell himself it was okay, nothing could make him stop missing Mum and Daisy.

Round and round the thoughts buzzed and battered, and try as he might, Fergus couldn't find any answers or, worse, get any sleep. Nervously, he checked the clock: 22:31 it read in luminous letters. Less than eight hours to go before they'd have to get up. This was ridiculous. He needed to rest. He needed to dream. He needed . . .

"Chimp!" he whispered.

The dog cocked an ear, then padded from the foot of the bed (where he'd ended up after all) to the pillow.

"Fancy a quick spin?" asked Fergus.

Chimp licked his face, which was all the reply Fergus needed.

"Come on," he said, pulling a jumper over his pyjamas and putting a pair of trainers on his feet. "Quick and quiet."

And for once, Chimp did exactly what he was told, and followed Fergus swiftly and softly out of the door.

Chapter 6

Place Your Bets

WHOMP!

"Ouch!"

"You great galah!"

Fergus and Chimp pulled
themselves out of Queen Woebegot's
prize rosebushes, picked prickles out
of their hands and paws, and made
their way to the back of the palace.

When they got there, it sounded as if someone else was in as much bother as Fergus was.

"How about a thousand dragons?" offered King Woebegot.

The king's brother, Duke Dastardly, clad all in black and with an even darker look on his face, scoffed. "A thousand dragons? What would I want with a thousand dragons?"

"Where would you even get a thousand dragons?" asked the queen. "That's what I'd like to know."

"Dragons 'R' Us," replied Unlucky Luke. "Second on the right on the ring road past Knight Supplies."

"Lawks-a-mussy," cried Queen Woebegot. "Whatever next? Horrible Hounds Holiday Park?"

"Oh, there's one of those out by Darklands Castle," replied Cousin Derek. "You should visit. There's an all-you-can-eat diner. For anyone who hasn't already been eaten, that is."

"Maybe that should be the booby prize," said Prince Waldorf. "A week trying to avoid hellish dogs."

"Steady on, mate," said Chimp.

"Fergus!" cried Princess Lily, turning to see her friend. "Maybe you can settle the bet?"

"This betting business is nonsense," said Hector.

Fergus frowned. His dad, the

Palace Pedallers' coach, seemed a little grumpy.

"It's not nonsense," insisted the king. "It's serious business."

"Well, if you want to get serious, why didn't you say?" demanded Duke Dastardly, giving his brother an evil look. "Dragons, schmagons. Let's make a proper bet. Winner gets . . . the loser's castle."

"What?" shouted the king.

"Orf with his head!" shrieked the queen. "Guards!"

"I don't think so, Deirdre." The duke smiled a slippery smile. "I am your brother-in-law, after all."

"Being family doesn't stop her," muttered the king. "She's tried to orf my head several times already this week, and I'm her husband."

"I like the idea," said Derek. "Two castles for me to rule."

"As if!" snapped Waldorf. "Two castles for us, you mean."

Fergus shook his head. In the bad old days Wallace's Winners and Hercules' Hopefuls had spent more time bickering than winning anything, but this lot were worse. If he wanted his own issues sorted,

clearly he'd have to help sort out
this argument first.

"Instead of winning a castle
forever," Fergus said, "why not just
get the loser's castle for a day?"

"Why?" demanded the duke.

"One day?" added the king.
"Where's the fun in that?"

"Well, where's the fun if you
lose your palace for good?" replied
Fergus. "Where would you live?"

"Fergus has got a point," his dad
agreed.

"Even better," continued Fergus,
"the prize is for the team captain.

Not the adults. So, if the Palace Pedallers win, Lily gets to be queen for the day. And if the Darklands Demons win, Derek is king for a day."

"And make up our own rules?" asked Derek.

Fergus nodded.

"Ooh, I like it," said Lily.

"Well, I don't," said Waldorf. "What about me? And besides, you can't be queen, Lily. I'm a boy so I'm first in line."

"But I was born first," said Lily.

"Boys rule," said Waldorf, shrugging. "Literally."

"Seriously?" asked Fergus, looking at his dad.

Hector nodded. "Never mind the Darklands. It's still the Dark Ages round here sometimes."

"Muuuu-uuuum?" wailed Lily. "Do something. And not 'orf' with anyone's head."

"Don't be silly, Lily," said her father. "Your mother agrees with me. She has to."

"Oh do I, indeed?"

Fergus looked on in astonishment as Queen Woebegot pointed her sceptre at her husband.

"I'm with Lily," she announced. "If that little team of hers wins, she'll be queen. It'll be good preparation for the future. Seeing as you'll be changing the law tomorrow morning, making girls as important as boys."

"Oh, will I?" asked the king, narrowing his eyes and adjusting his crown.

"Yes, you *will*," retorted the queen, glaring fiercely and adjusting her own bigger crown.

"Oh, very well then, dear," said the king, looking sheepish.

Lily and Fergus high-fived. They'd done it!

"Brilliotic!" yelled Lily.

"Too right!" agreed Fergus.

"Er, aren't you bozos forgetting something?" asked Chimp.

"What's that?"

"The race?" he said. "You haven't actually won yet."

Lily gulped. Fergus pulled a
face. Chimp was right. Never
mind tomorrow's Internationals in
Manchester. Today was the final of
the Nevermore Tournament, and the
Palace Pedallers had to win. Not just
so Lily could be queen for a day. It
was more important than that.

So that King Woebegot finally
accepted girls were as brilliant as
boys, and that, one day, Lily might
be queen of Nevermore for good.

Chapter 7

Ruler for a Day

As the teams lined up and made last-minute adjustments to their kit, Fergus thought again about the whole hoo-hah in Nevermore: how bicycles had been banned, how his dad had been banished and then imprisoned, and how hard it had been pleading with King and Queen Woebegot to let Lily and Waldorf even try cycling again. But now there was a chance that Lily might be officially allowed to inherit the castle. This race just *had* to go well.

At least this time there were no wizards trying to cast spells on the cyclists, or dragons trying to destroy the track. No, this race was down to just two things: talent and determination. The Palace Pedallers

had plenty of both, but so did Derek and his teammates Nigel, Norman and Norris – the Darklands Demons.

Yes, thought Fergus to himself as the starting pistol was raised, this was going to be a race to remember, all right.

"Come on, Lily!" called Fergus as the racers took the first turn. "Give those Demons a licking."

"Demons?" Chimp joined in. "Drongos, more like. And I wouldn't lick them in a month of Sundays."

"It means beat them in the race," Fergus explained. "Not actually lick them!"

Chimp clapped a paw over his eyes. "I know! I was joking, mate."

"I don't think we've got time for jokes," hissed Hector. "Check out Scary Mary."

Fergus looked back at the track to see Nigel, Norris and Norman all swerve in front of Mary in perfect triangle formation, pushing her into a barrier.

"One down, Derek!" called Duke Dastardly. "You'll be making up rules in minutes." He cackled horribly.

"Don't you believe it," called back King Woebegot. "My Lily's still leagues ahead. She'll be the one bossing your boy about, mark my words."

"You're sure about that?" asked the duke, as Unlucky Luke found himself next in line for the triangle treatment.

"Foul!" called the queen. "Orf with their heads!"

"Fair!" replied the duke. "Orf with yours!"

Queen Woebegot puffed herself up like an angry cat. "No one tells *me* what to do!" she snapped.

Duke Dastardly smiled. "Give it five minutes and you might find that's changed."

More like two minutes, thought Fergus as the remaining riders

rounded the back straight. Lily was
neck and neck with Derek, and
Waldorf was bringing up the rear,
chased by the rest of the Darklands
Demons, who were already eyeing
up their next target.

"Look out, Waldorf!" called
Fergus. "They're behind you."

"Oh, no they're not!" shouted the
duke.

"Oh, yes they are!" shouted the
queen.

And they were. But Waldorf was
ready, and before they could do the

triangle trick to him Waldorf had
swung off to the left, leaving them
heading straight for the barrier
themselves.

Whomp! Whomp! Whomp!

One by one, Nigel, Norris and
Norman hit the buffers, then the
ground.

"Woo-hoo, Waldorf! Go, Pedallers!" yelled Fergus.

"Go, Lily, more like," Chimp said, pointing with a paw at the track.

"You're not wrong," Fergus admitted. Waldorf was way behind now, after seeing off the three Demons, and as Lily and Derek headed into the last lap, it was clear this race was now a head-to-head.

"Go, Lily," Fergus urged, crossing everything he could think to cross. "Don't let Derek take the crown!"

"For real," agreed Chimp. "Imagine the laws he'll invent."

"No talking dogs?" suggested Fergus.

Chimp crossed his paws and huffed.

"My turn to joke," said Fergus, giving his pal a pat. "But it is the final straight, so maybe save it for later?"

Chimp mimed zipping his mouth. Fergus did the same. Along with them, the whole crowd who had gathered to watch fell silent as Derek and Lily started to sprint for the finish line.

Go on, Lily, Fergus said in his head, too tense to shout out loud. *Do this for the Pedallers. And for girls. And for cycling itself!*

As if his words were carried on
the wind, over the crowd, along the
track and into Lily's head, no sooner
had Fergus thought them, Lily dug
deep and pushed down hard on the
pedals.

Fergus saw she was pushing
harder than she'd ever done before.

Lily pulled ahead of Derek.

"Nooooooo!" called the duke.

"Yeeeeeees!" called the king.

"Yeeeeeees!" echoed Fergus,
Hector and Chimp as Lily slipped
over the finish line with seconds
to spare.

"She's done it!" whooped
Luke, who had recovered from
his fall, along with Scary Mary,
who enthusiastically nodded her
agreement.

"Hurrah for Lily!" called King
Woebegot.

"Long live Queen Lily!" quipped the queen.

"Queen? Pah!" spat Duke Dastardly, decidedly downhearted.

Prince Derek yanked off his helmet, and slammed his own crown back on. "Only for a day," he muttered. "And I won't be abiding by any of her rules, whatever anyone says."

"Orf with his head!" demanded Queen Woebegot.

"No, not orf with anything," said Lily. "I'm giving the orders now, remember?" Then she glared at Derek. "And you don't even know what I *am* going to say."

"So what is it then?" her cousin asked. "Boys to be banned from racing? Girls to get the best bikes?"

"No chocolate pudding for brothers?" asked Waldorf, with a worried air.

Lily laughed. "You're both daft," she said. "I've only got three rules. One, girls can become queen. Two . . ." she turned to Fergus, nodding at him to take over.

Fergus grinned. He knew what she wanted.

"Two, cycling to be made a protected sport, so it can never be outlawed again." He looked at Lily for approval, and got it back in a wink.

"And last of all," continued Lily, "rule three: I don't have to be queen when I'm grown up if I don't want to."

"Why wouldn't you want to?" demanded Derek.

It was Lily's turn to grin. "Isn't it obvious? Because I'll have far better things to do being in charge of the national cycle team, as well as being their number one racer!"

"Yes!" said Fergus, delighted. He grinned at his dad and Hector grinned back.

"Well, I suppose . . ." King Woebegot agreed.

"Orf with nobody's heads!" cried Queen Woebegot. "And now it's time for tea at the palace. If Queen Lily agrees, of course?"

"Of course," Lily replied. "Only no chocolate pudding for Waldorf."

Her brother's face fell.

"Joke!" she said, then turned to Fergus. "Coming?"

Fergus shook his head. "Actually, I was going to ask you the same thing."

"What?" Lily looked confused.

"Just . . . well, it's the Internationals in the morning and Mum can't come and nor can Daisy and I wondered . . . " His voice trailed off.

Lily smiled. "Oh, Fergie. I'd love to. But Dad'll be back in charge by then, and me and Waldorf aren't allowed out of Nevermore until we're at least eighteen."

"Oh." Fergus felt his heart sigh and his stomach slump. "Okay then."

"But I'll see you soon?" Lily asked.

Fergus nodded. "Aye," he said, sadly, still feeling disappointed. "I expect so."

Lily gave him a quick hug and hurried off to oversee afternoon tea, leaving Fergus to say his goodbyes to his dad.

"You'll ride a blinder in the Internationals, Fergus," Hector said. "I just know it. If that's what you're worried about."

"I don't suppose . . .?" began Fergus, a seed of hope taking root.

"I can't," said his dad before Fergus could finish. "You know that. Besides, your mum's about to get married. I'm the last person she needs to turn up and surprise her."

"But she's being weird," Fergus blurted then. "She's off her food, and she's tired all the time, and she won't come to Manchester and she won't say why and it's not just work, I know it."

His dad was frowning, but slowly, as he listened to Fergus, a smile spread across his face instead. "Off her food, you say? And tired? Och, sonny," Hector said. "I'm pretty sure your mum is right as rain. You just stop your worrying and get on with racing. If I remember

Jeanie right, that's what she'd want."

"Really?" Fergus asked. "You're not just saying that?"

"Really," Hector replied. "I know I'm your dad and I'm supposed to say stuff like that, but it's true. Ride like the wind, son. For me. For your mum. And for Lily and Daisy too."

Fergus felt the seed of happiness sprout, and his heart sing with it. His dad knew what to say to make him feel better, even if he couldn't come and watch him in the Internationals.

"I will ride like the wind," he promised. "I absolutely will."

"Now get going," Hector said.

"I'm gone," said Fergus.

And he was. Back to his bike, back into the sky with Chimp, and back to his bunk in the Manchester Grand, where, at 10.32pm precisely, he quickly fell into a deep and dreamless sleep.

Chapter 8

The International Finish Line

"I feel sick," said Wesley, staring queasily at his porridge on the morning of their third and final day.

"I'm not surprised," Choppy told his son, as he tucked into eggs and bacon himself. "Second in the knock-out to the Brisbane Belters, and neck and neck with the Shanghai Shooting Stars after yesterday. There's everything to play for."

After the road race and the knock-out race, Hercules' Hopefuls were in the top three and the pressure was on. Doing well in the team track final that day was crucial.

"It's just nerves," Fergus reassured Wesley, eating his own breakfast with gusto. "We all get them."

"Well, not me," said Wesley. "I must be ill. Or poisoned!" He eyed Bruce Hunter from the Brisbane Belters, sitting opposite them, with suspicion.

"Och, Wesley, your imagination is as wild as our Fergie's at times." Grandpa laughed. "Now, get that porridge down you. You've a race to run. And I've a bet to win," he added, nodding at someone on the far side of the restaurant.

"Who's that?" asked Fergus.

"Major Margaret Menzies," said Choppy.

"From the Velociraptors?" Wesley demanded, nerves (and poison) forgotten.

"Aye," said Choppy. "Herc's fancy lady."

"Och, she is not," insisted Grandpa. "We've just a little bet going on, remember?"

Fergus nodded. He did remember: double or quits to win the Internationals. Well, Fergus would be racing for the team's glory first. But winning the bet might come in handy, what with the wedding. Mum and Jambo had certainly seemed worried about having enough money lately.

"Come on, Hopefuls," he said, pushing his chair back with a screech. "Time to get sweaty!"

"Half an hour's rest!" warned Choppy. "Give your food time to go down."

"Then we want you back at the track, warmed up and in full kit," said Grandpa. "You too." He nodded at Mikey and Calamity, the reserves, as well as Dermot, who wasn't on the team sheet for the race, but was still part of the squad.

Just like Daisy. *Once a Hopeful, always a Hopeful*, Fergus thought.

As Fergus made his way back to the bedroom to get changed, he tried to push aside his sadness at Daisy's absence. But the thought of his best friend lingered as he pulled on his Hopefuls jersey.

And as he pulled up his Hopefuls
socks. And even as he pulled tight
the strap on his Hopefuls helmet.

Fergus felt a pat on his back and
turned to see Wesley.

"You can do it without her," he
said.

Wesley, of all people, knew what
Fergus was thinking!

Surprised, Fergus nodded. "I
know," he said. "But it won't be the
same."

"But it'll still be brilliant, right?"

Fergus paused. Wesley was
right. He had to focus on the good

stuff. "Better than brilliant," he said eventually, finding a smile. "It'll be –"

"Brilliotic!"

This time, both Fergus and Wesley turned, and both found themselves with mouths wide open with shock.

"Daisy!" they chorused.

"What? Did you think I'd let you get all the glory for yourself?" Daisy said with a grin.

"B-b-but –" blustered Fergus.

"Butts are for sitting on," said Daisy. "You know that, Fergus Hamilton. Now come on, your mum's downstairs – she got the train this morning. Sorcha's with her too – her parents picked me up on the way back from their holiday in the Hebrides, before you ask."

Fergus grinned. This was brilliotic! Better than brilliotic, even.

So with his arms around Wesley and Daisy, and Chimp hopping excitedly at his heels, Fergus made

his way towards the biggest race of
his life.

If the race was big, the stadium
was bigger. The velodrome was
incredible – steep, sloped sides
and a track so long it seemed to
disappear into the distance. It made
Middlebank look tiny in comparison.
All around them was the crowd,
from the die-hard fans in the front
row to the cameras flashing in the
press area and journalists sending
reports halfway round the world,
and all the children high up in the
stands, hoping that, one day, it
would be them out there on the
track.

Right where Fergus was.

Sitting there on his saddle on the starting line, Fergus had never felt so . . . small. So insignificant. Did Spokes Sullivan feel like this? Surely not! He had everyone cheering for him.

But then Fergus realised something: the crowd might be massive, a sea of unfamiliar faces, thousands of them, but in there, somewhere, were people cheering just for him. People who, alongside his team-mates, mattered more than anything in the world.

With that he felt a surge of hope, and with it, want. He wanted to do this – for all of them. He gave one last look at the concentration on the faces of his team. They were all ready, looking determined.

"On your marks!" came the
call, echoing around the incredible
velodrome.

Fergus lowered himself over the
handlebars, blocking out the sight
of the spectators and the other
competitors, focusing on the sound
of his own heartbeat.

"Get set!"

Fergus poised his right foot on
the pedal.

"GO!"

And with that, Fergus pushed
down as hard as he could and sped
off to a flying start. As they took
the turn into the back straight, only
Bruce Hunter from the Brisbane
Belters and Ken Cho from the
Shanghai Shooting Stars were ahead
of him.

It was hard going. The banked
wooden track was very different
to the cinder one at Carnoustie
Common, and even the tarmac at
Middlebank hadn't prepared him
for the Manchester velodrome. Even
though he'd had a good night's sleep

and a decent breakfast inside him,
Fergus found himself struggling
to keep pace. Maybe the Hopefuls
have been kidding themselves all
along, he thought. Maybe they were
the best in Scotland. But in the
world? It wasn't looking likely.

Glancing behind quickly, Fergus
could see that Belinda was level
pegging with the French number one
in fifth place, but Wesley was way
back in the pack, as was Minnie.
As they hit the last lap, they were
looking to lose those places.

Fergus's stomach plummeted. This
was terrible. What a fool he'd been
thinking he could compete at this
level. He wasn't a winner. He'd not
had years of top-level training or

the world's flashiest kit. He was just
a kid from a back street in Scotland.

Hopeful? Hopeless, more like.

But then . . .

"Go on, Fergus!" came the yell,
though he couldn't tell if it was
from Mum or Daisy or one of the
amazing number of strangers who
had come out to support the Scots
team.

"Eyes on the prize!"

That was definitely Grandpa.
Knowing he was riding for such loyal
fans and family gave Fergus the
boost he needed. As they rounded
the corner into the final straight,

Fergus dug deep inside, deeper than he had ever done, to find that extra energy. All his thoughts pulled back from the track and into his imagination.

And that's when it happened.

"Keep going, Fergus," he heard. "You're flying!"

He felt his heart pound quicker.

It couldn't be, could it? Only, it sounded just like . . . Lily.

"Go on, son. You're really flying!"

Dad!

Fergus couldn't look, couldn't

take his eyes off the race in front of him. But no matter who had said it, Fergus felt it. He was flying – even though his wheels were firmly on the track!

Fergus raced right past Bruce Hunter, who let out a "No!" as he passed, then there were only inches between him and Ken Cho, and only metres to go.

"Go on!" yelled the crowd. "You can do it!"

"I can!" Fergus told himself. "I can do it! I can . . . "

And Fergus flew over the finish line, knowing in his heart that he absolutely had done it.

He'd pushed himself and done his best, and the feeling was out of this world.

It had been a photo finish in the end, with Ken Cho and the Shanghai Shooting Stars just pipping Fergus and the Hopefuls to gold. But as he stood on the podium with his team-mates, silver medals on their chests, hearts puffed with pride, Fergus couldn't have been happier.

Out there in the crowd was Grandpa, holding Chimp up for a wave. There was Mum, her arms around Jambo. There were Daisy and Sorcha, one end of a homemade "Go Hopefuls!" banner each. And there were . . . Fergus scanned the stands again, in case he'd missed them.

But Dad and Lily were nowhere to be seen.

So he closed his eyes.

"Nice one, son," said Dad.

Lily grinned. "We knew you'd do us proud."

Fergus grinned too, and opened his eyes again as the cameras flashed and the national anthem of the People's Republic of China played.

So the Hercules' Hopefuls hadn't won gold. And Grandpa had lost his bet. But Fergus had won silver in the International Championships, after less than a year in the saddle. He'd done his team, his family and his friends proud.

He really had pulled it off.

In this world and in Nevermore.

Chapter 9

Two of a Kind

"Are you sure you need another slice of cake?" signed Sorcha.

Fergus nodded, cramming the cream and sponge into his mouth.

"You won't be able to dance," signed Sorcha.

"Good!" Fergus signed back, swallowing as he did so.

This wedding was a dancer of a day, but having to do the hokey-cokey might just ruin the moment. And Fergus didn't want anything to mess with this moment.

Not only had Mum changed her mind about itchy suits, tight ties and sticky-out bridesmaid dresses to let him and all his friends attend in the Hercules' Hopefuls team strip, but there'd been no daftly expensive cake, no posh photographer and no having to sing hymns he couldn't remember the words to.

The "make do and mend" idea had been Grandpa's. With Fergus's help (and Chimp's hindrance, snaffling cocktail sausages as fast as they could plate them up), Jambo had

made the buffet tea, Daisy and
Sorcha had made the cake and
Grandpa had decorated the hall
with the help of his friend, Major
Margaret Menzies.

"She's not my fancy lady," Grandpa
insisted to Fergus. "But I didn't
have the cash to honour the bet,
so I invited her here for a day out
instead. You've got to admit, she's
pretty canny with the carnations."

Fergus looked around at the regimented flower arrangements, as neat and orderly as the Velociraptors themselves. "Aye," he agreed.

"Though I wish she'd stop putting the sausage rolls into rows," said Daisy. "I like my food precarious."

Fergus looked at the teetering pile of pork pie, jam tart and jelly on Daisy's plate. "No dancing for you either, I reckon," he said.

"Maybe a little spin later, though?" she asked, miming pedalling a bicycle.

"Can I come?" Sorcha signed.

Fergus looked oddly at Sorcha. Had he understood her right?

Sorcha saw his look and wrote on her pad:

You heard me.

Can I come with you?

Fergus frowned. Sorcha had never seemed that interested in going cycling herself. She'd always watched the races with them, but riding had always been Fergus's thing with Daisy. He felt a little awkward and looked over at Daisy.

But Daisy simply grinned. Then, together, Fergus and Daisy did the new sign they'd made up especially: "Brilliotic!"

Sorcha signed it back: "Brilliotic!"

"We'll be needing a new member, after all," added Grandpa. "Unless you're planning on becoming a stowaway, Daisy?"

Daisy shook her head. "I've a trial next Friday for the Inverness Arrows. My friends Jack and Ryan are on the squad, and they reckon I'm in with a good chance of a place. So maybe I'll see you on the track at next year's Nationals."

"You'll see my dust, more like," said Fergus with a smile.

"You wish," said Daisy. But she was smiling too, and so was Sorcha, and so, in fact, was everyone.

Everyone, that is, except Mum.

Fergus looked over at the bride as she talked to Mrs MacCafferty. Mum was happy, sure. In fact, Fergus had never seen her happier than when Jambo said, "I do!" and the whole room had erupted into whoops of joy.

But something was up, and Fergus was determined to get to the bottom of it.

"Here," he said, handing Mum a piece of Daisy's cake as she sat down at the top table.

"Och, no, love." His mum pushed it away, and put a hand on her belly.

"Have you eaten too much?" Fergus asked, concerned. "Or maybe it's just the excitement? Or are you worried about the icing dropping on your white dress? I know you'd rather have your jeans on."

"Maybe I should have come in my nurse's uniform," Mum joked then. But she still wasn't laughing. "It's not that anyway," she said.

"Jeanie?" Jambo said, sitting down beside his wife. "Have you told him?"

"Not yet," Mum said. "I was waiting."

"Waiting for what?" Fergus demanded, feeling suddenly worried again. "Tell me what? What's going on?"

"Hey, hey," Jambo said, putting his arm on Fergus to calm him down.

But Fergus was far from calm. "Something's wrong, isn't it?" he said. "Are we moving? Is that it? Or is one of you ill? Or . . . or . . . is there an alien invasion?" Fergus's big imagination began to take hold. "Or is a secret super-villain sidekick about to brainwash Scotland into believing Evil McWeevil should be First Minister?"

At that, Mum's mouth cracked a smile. "Och, Fergie," she said. "You really are one of a kind, you know that?"

"You too," he said. "So please don't be ill." He stared at his mum

with worry that wouldn't go away
written on his face.

"Fergie, no one's ill. There are
no aliens, either," added Jambo.
"Or . . . what was the other one?
That's right, super-villains. But
we do have some news."

He nodded at Jeanie, who looked
at Fergus.

"I meant what I said," she told
him. "You're one of a kind, Fergus.
Only . . . well, you might have to get
used to sharing a bit."

"Sharing what?" asked Fergus. "I
already share everything with Chimp.
I don't think we can afford enough
sausages for another dog."

"It's not a dog," said Mum. "I meant that you'll have to get used to sharing me."

"With Jambo?" asked Fergus, relief flooding him with warmth. "No problem."

"Well, not just with me, son," said
Jambo. "You see, the thing is . . ."

The cake in Fergus's tummy began
to churn.

"Yes," continued Mum. "The thing
is . . . "

"What is the thing?" cried Fergus
impatiently.

Mum took a deep breath, and
pulled a black and white photo from
her white handbag. "Fergus Horatio
Hamilton," she said, "meet your
brother."

Fergus stared at the photo. What
was this? A brother he'd never heard
of? It looked more like a baked bean.

Or an alien, after all.

Then he got it. This was a hospital scan! Which meant this wasn't an alien. Or a baked bean.

This was a baby!

Mum was *pregnant*! That explained why she'd been tired and feeling sick and worried about money. No one was moving anywhere. But everything was changing. And fast.

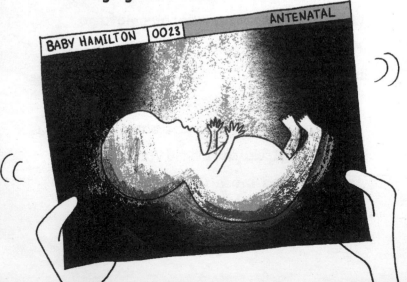

"Fergie?" asked Mum. "Are you feeling okay?"

Fergus wasn't sure. He was certainly feeling something. A sort of strange tingling all over.

Maybe he'd eaten too much cake.

Or maybe this baby was going to be the end of the world. I mean, who'd have time for him once a brother arrived?

But no sooner than he'd said that word – brother – to himself, Fergus knew exactly what he was feeling.

"Brilliotic!" he said. "A baby brother! This is absolutely the best thing ever!"

"Well, maybe not better than silver at the Internationals," Mum pointed out, laughing.

"Maybe not," admitted Fergus. "But it's a photo finish, for sure!"

As Fergus lay in bed that night, in his right hand a wedding photo of him, Mum and Jambo grinning at the camera, and in his left hand the scan photo of his brand new baby brother, Fergus really did feel brilliotic.

Things were about to change, but he could handle it. He had Sorcha to talk to. And Daisy was only at the end of the telephone line too. And then there were his

team-mates, here and in Nevermore:
Lily and Belinda, both feisty and
fun; Wesley and Waldorf who
could wind him up until the cows
came home; Minnie and Mikey the
bickering brother and sister; Unlucky
Luke and Calamity, who'd had more
than their fair share of accidents
between them; Scary Mary who had
yet to say a word to him; and finally
Dermot, who was difficult at best,
and dimwitted at worst, but utterly
indispensible.

Fergus wondered what Dad would
have to say about the news when
he told him. But then again, maybe
Dad already knew. And besides,
that was a conversation for another
day.

No, Fergus thought, as he put down the pictures and switched off the light, *things really couldn't get any better.*

Although he wouldn't say no to gold next year . . .

Sir Chris Hoy MBE, won his first Olympic gold medal in Athens 2004. Four years later in Beijing he became the first Briton since 1908 to win three gold medals in a single Olympic Games. In 2012, Chris won two gold medals at his home Olympics in London, becoming Britain's most successful Olympian with six gold medals and one silver. Sir Chris also won eleven World titles and two Commonwealth Games gold medals. In December 2008, Chris was voted BBC Sports Personality of the Year, and he received a Knighthood in the 2009 New Year Honours List. Sir Chris retired as a professional competitive cyclist in early 2013; he still rides almost daily. He lives in Manchester with his family.

www.chrishoy.com

Joanna Nadin is an award-winning author of
more than seventy books for children, including
the bestselling Rachel Riley diaries, the Penny
Dreadful series, and Joe All Alone, now a BAFTA
award-winning TV series. She studied drama and
politics at university in Hull and London, and has
worked as a lifeguard, a newsreader and even a
special adviser to the Prime Minister. She now
teaches writing and lives in Bath, where she rides
her rickety bicycle, but she never, ever back-
pedals...

www.joannanadin.com

Clare Elsom is an illustrator of lots of lovely children's books, including Maisie Mae and the Spies in Disguise series. She is also the author-illustrator of Horace and Harriet. She studied Illustration at Falmouth University (lots of drawing) and Children's Literature at Roehampton University (lots of writing). Clare lives in Devon, where she can be found doodling, tap dancing and drinking cinnamon lattes.

www.elsomillustration.co.uk

This brilliotic book about Fergus and his friends is set in a reader-friendly font and design, for maximum enjoyment for everyone.

The font we have used is called OpenDyslexic. You can find out more about it here: **www.opendyslexic.org**

Dyslexia affects as many as 1 in 10 people, and often makes reading more difficult. We wanted to make our books as easy to enjoy as possible, so this special font and a design with lots of space helps us do just that.

Not everyone with difficulty reading has dyslexia, and not everyone with dyslexia has the same difficulties. You can find out more about dyslexia on these wonderful websites:

The Dyslexia Association: **dyslexia.uk.net**

British Dyslexia Assocation: **bdadyslexia.org.uk**

Dyslexia Scotland: **www.dyslexiascotland.org.uk**

Piccadilly
PRESS

Thank you for choosing a Piccadilly Press book.

If you would like to know more about our authors, our books or if you'd just like to know what we're up to, you can find us online.

www.piccadillypress.co.uk

You can also find us on:

We hope to see you soon!